Little Red Ruthie

A Hanukkah Tale

Gloria Koster

pictures by
Sue Eastland

Albert Whitman & Company
Chicago, Illinois

In loving memory of my mother,
Hella Ebner Bussel, who gave me the gift
of fairy tales once upon a time—GK

To my lovely, funny Yasmin—SE

Library of Congress Cataloging-in-Publication data is on file with the publisher.

Text copyright © 2017 by Gloria Koster
Pictures copyright © 2017 by Albert Whitman & Company
Pictures by Sue Eastland
Published in 2017 by Albert Whitman & Company
ISBN 978-0-8075-4646-8

Printed in China
10 9 8 7 6 5 4 3 2 1 HH 22 21 20 19 18 17

Design by Morgan Avery

For more information about Albert Whitman & Company,
visit our website at www.albertwhitman.com.

It was a chilly winter in the northern woods, but Ruthie did not mind. Every year she and her grandmother made latkes together for Hanukkah. Today she was on her way to Bubbe Basha's house on the other side of the forest.

Ruthie was taking sour cream and applesauce to go along with the yummy potato pancakes they would make. She carefully packed her basket and kissed her mother good-bye.

"Stay safe, my Little Red Ruthie, and stick to the path."

"I promise, Mommy," she said. She skipped along the trail.

Snow began to fall. Soon a white blanket covered the ground, causing Ruthie to lose her way. Suddenly something jumped out from behind a tree. Ruthie found herself face-to-face with a wolf!

"Little girl," said the wolf,
"I am going to...*eat you up!*"

Ruthie's heart raced. Her tummy flip-flopped.
But she could not let the wolf know she was scared.
It was Hanukkah, and Ruthie wanted to be brave
as the Maccabees.

Being a clever girl, she offered a smart and speedy reply. "Mr. Wolf," she explained, "underneath my puffy coat, I am actually skinny as a twig. But I'm on my way to cook latkes with my Bubbe Basha.

"Each day of Hanukkah, I plan to eat a plateful of delicious potato pancakes. When the holiday is over, I am sure to be as round as a pancake myself. If you wait just eight days, you are guaranteed to have a better meal. Why not eat me then?"

Her words were so enticing, the wolf agreed. He even led her out of the thicket and back onto the trail.

But his stomach began to rumble. In the distance, his tasty morsel was disappearing. "Deal's off!" he declared, leaping through the forest and arriving at Bubbe Basha's cottage before Ruthie. Perhaps he would eat the grandmother first.

There was a note on the door.

Dear Ruthie,
I went to the village to buy us a Hanukkah treat. I will be back soon.

OOOXXX

Bubbe Basha

The wolf could not read. Finding no one at home was a big disappointment. While waiting for Ruthie to arrive, he entertained himself by trying on some of Bubbe Basha's clothes, admiring himself in the mirror.

Ruthie, on the other hand, was an excellent reader. Learning that her grandmother was running an errand, she was surprised to see a light inside the cottage. She peered through the window and recognized the wolf. I must be brave as the Maccabees, she reminded herself, pushing aside a wave of fear. Ruthie greeted the wolf like an old friend.

"Mr. Wolf, how hungry you must be to come all this way. Before you gobble me up, allow me to fry up a platter of luscious latkes. Once I am gone, you won't have the chance to enjoy their heavenly taste."

That sounded delightful. But the wolf was used to eating his food raw. "Hurry up," he demanded, "and skip the frying part!"

"We can't," Ruthie insisted. "A latke is not a latke unless it's fried. Oil is very important in the Hanukkah story!" Nobody had ever shared a story with the wolf. So Ruthie told him the tale of the Maccabees' victory.

"When the Maccabees took back their temple," she explained, "they discovered a tiny bit of oil. Nobody believed it could provide light for more than one day, but it lasted for eight days. That is the Hanukkah miracle. And that is why you must wait while I prepare a treat that is crispy on the outside and silky smooth on the inside."

The wolf was an impatient sort, but he agreed. He even sat down at the kitchen table, where Bubbe Basha had already laid out the ingredients—potatoes, onions, eggs, and flour.

Ruthie was thankful for all the times she and her grandmother had made latkes together, but could she make them on her own?

As she worked, Ruthie found she remembered the entire recipe by heart! Soon the irresistible aroma of the sizzling latkes filled the room.

"Aren't they ready yet?" whined the hungry wolf.

By the time Ruthie served him a stack of potato pancakes, drool was dripping down his chin. He ate a plateful and then another...

and another...

Bubbe Basha returned, horrified to see Ruthie in danger. Fortunately the wolf was now full up to his eyeballs and very groggy.

"Bubbe," said Ruthie, "our guest has been munching on some latkes, but it is surely time for his main course."

"N-n-n-no, thank you," stammered the wolf.
He wanted nothing more than some fresh forest
air and headed for the door.

"What a pity you must leave," said Bubbe Basha. "But we can't send you on your way without a treat."

She reached into her bag, pulled out a jelly doughnut, and placed it in the wolf's paw. "Enjoy this tomorrow," she said, ushering him outside.

Ruthie breathed a sigh of relief.

After plenty of hugs and kisses, Ruthie and her grandmother lit the first Hanukkah candle and sat down at the table.

Thanks to Little Red Ruthie, dinner was ready, and it was delicious.

Ruthie's Potato Latke Recipe

Latkes so good a big bad wolf will eat them up instead of you!

6 medium potatoes

1 small onion finely chopped

1 large egg, beaten

¼ cup flour

½ teaspoon salt

pinch of pepper to taste

oil for frying

Peel and grate the potatoes. Place them in a bowl of cold water to keep them from turning brown. Drain the potatoes and spread them onto a towel with the chopped onions. Roll up the towel and squeeze out as much moisture as you can. Transfer the potatoes and onions to a large bowl and mix together with the egg, flour, salt, and pepper.

With the help of an adult, cover the bottom of a large skillet with cooking oil. Heat on high. Drop 2–3 tablespoons of the mixture per latke into the oil and flatten with the back of a spoon. Lower the heat to medium. Fry for about 3–4 minutes on each side or until the latkes are golden brown and crispy. Place them on paper towels to drain. Continue cooking the remaining mixture, adding more oil as needed.

Serve warm with sour cream, applesauce, or any yummy topping of your choice.